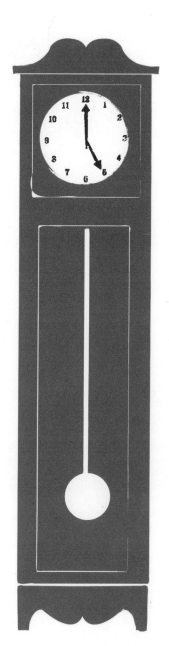

For Mattie and Bill

www.alisonmurray.net

ORCHARD BOOKS
338 Euston Road, London NW1 3BH
Orchard Books Australia
Level 17/207 Kent Street, Sydney, NSW 2000

First published in 2012 by Orchard Books

ISBN 978 1 40831 198 1

Text and illustrations © Alison Murray 2012

The right of Alison Murray to be identified as the author and illustrator
of this work has been asserted by her in accordance with the
Copyrights, Designs and Patents Act, 1988.

2 4 6 8 10 9 7 5 3 1

A CIP catalogue record for this book is available from the British Library.

Printed in China

Orchard Books is a division of Hachette Children's Books, an Hachette UK company.

www.hachette.co.uk

Hickory Dickory DOG

Alison Murray

ORCHARD

Hickory, dickory, dock,
A dog, a boy . . .

. . . a clock!

The day's begun,

It's time for fun!

Hickory, dickory, dock.

Hickory, dickory, dear, Rufus has to stay here.

There's a whine and a pine,

And a wet paint sign. Hickory, dickory, dear.

Hickory, dickory, dare,

NO DOGS ALLOWED

Dogs aren't allowed in there.
A sneaky peek through . . .

Then a **hullabaloo!**

Hickory, dickory, dare.

Hickory, dickory, dee,

Haroo!

Hurrah!

Yippee!

The clock strikes eleven,

It's make-a-mess heaven!

Hickory, dickory, dee.

Hickory, lickery, lunch.
Some yummy crumbs to munch.

The clock strikes noon,

Zac's dropped his spoon!
Hickory, lickery, lunch.

Hickory, dickory, doo.
Uh-oh! A gloop of glue!

The weather is fine ...

. . . so it's garden time.

Hickory, dickory, doo.

Hickory, stickory, stack.
A scritchety, scratchety back.

Time is up, you mucky pup!
Hickory, stickory, stack.

Higglety, pigglety, pup.
It's home to clean you up!

The clock strikes five.

Slip,

Slide,

Crash . . .

. . . Dive!

Higglety, pigglety, pup.

Hickory, flickory, fly. Rufus still needs to get dry.

First a bit of an itch.

Then a twist and a twitch.

Hickory, flickory, fly.

Hickory, dickory, dock.

A dog, a boy, a clock.

Now, it's time
For the end of the rhyme . . .

Hickory, dickory, dog.